good deed rain

50 Books by Allen Frost

...Ohio Trio...Bowl of Water...Another Life...
...Home Recordings...The Mermaid Translation...
...The Selected Correspondence of Kenneth
Patchen...The Wonderful Stupid Man...
...Saint Lemonade...Playground...Roosevelt...
...5 Novels...The Sylvan Moore Show...
...Town in a Cloud...A Flutter of Birds Passing
Through Heaven: A Tribute to Robert Sund...
..At the Edge of America..Lake Erie Submarine..
...The Book of Ticks...I Can Only Imagine...
...The Orphanage of Abandoned Teenagers...
..Different Planet..Go With the Flow: A Tribute
to Clyde Sanborn...Homeless Sutra...
..The Lake Walker..A Hundred Dreams Ago..
..Almost Animals..The Robotic Age..Kennedy..
...Fable...Elbows & Knees: Essays and Plays...
...The Last Paper Stars...Walt Amherst is Awake...
....When You Smile You Let in Light....
...Pinocchio in America...Florida...
..Blue Anthem Wailing..The Welfare Office..
...Island Air...Imaginary Someone...
....Violet of the Silent Movies....
...The Tin Can Telephone...Heaven Crayon...
..Old Salt..A Field of Cabbages..River Road..
...The Puttering Marvel...Something Bright...
...The Trillium Witch...Cosmonaut...
...Thriftstore Madonna...Half a Giraffe...

G
I
R
A
F
F
E

F
a
L
A
H

HALF A GIRAFFE © 2021
Allen Frost, Good Deed Rain
Bellingham, Washington
ISBN 978-1-0880-0585-9

Writing: Allen Frost
Cover Photo: San Diego giraffe we knew
Interior Drawings: Allen Frost
Cover Production: Fred Sodt
Apple: TFK!

HALF A GIRAFFE

Allen Frost

Good Deed Rain ◊ Bellingham, Washington ◊ 2021

"I've never known a mean butterfly in my life."
—Ray Goulding

The CHAPTERS

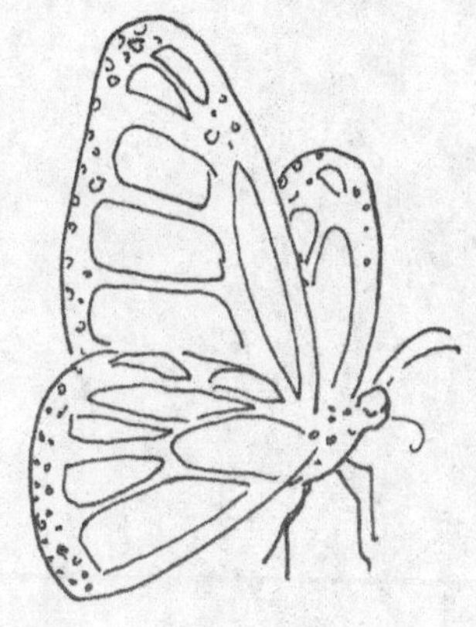

CHAPTER 1
The BIRTHDAY PARTY

This summer I got a giraffe. I didn't ask for it. I certainly didn't go looking for it. But she found me just the same.

She's out there in the yard. As long as the weather stays this hot, she doesn't mind. At night she stands there like a tree.

Where do you even get a giraffe? I know how I got mine. It was out of the blue. I'll tell you in a minute. First let me introduce myself. I'm Virgil Chef.

Let's see...what else...I'm 54 years old if that matters, I'm self-employed, I live in a little house on Mill Avenue and it's not like I'm a giraffe expert. I'm learning to be one. I go to the library and get books on the subject. I would tell you more, but there's someone at the door. I better see what they want. Whoever they are, they mean business.

It's not far from my chair to the front door. Less than ten paces anyway. I recognized the face in the little window. My neighbor. He doesn't look happy. I don't think he wants to borrow some sugar.

"Hello, Rocko," I said pleasantly.

He got right to the point. "Your giraffe is eating my kid's piñata!"

"What are you talking about?"

"Go look! It's ruining the birthday party!" His hands were balled up in fists. "That thing's a menace!"

"Okay, okay. I'll go take a look. I'll see what I can do," I said. "Thanks for letting me know." I shut the door and made my way through the room, through the kitchen to the back door. I can't keep an eye on the giraffe all the time. I have a life to live.

The sun shined on the backyard, the yellow grass blistered, the tall wooden fence kept everything captured. I saw my giraffe with her head leaned over the fence, reaching into the next-door neighbor's yard. The kids were still screaming. She was gnawing at a big paper star hanging from their tree.

"Tulip!" I said, "Let go of that!"

Her ear twitched and she turned in my direction. A trail of painted newsprint hung from her mouth. She doesn't need to forage over there. I make sure she gets all the food she needs, a variety of fruit and vegetables in season, fresh acacia leaves, hay, and special high-fiber biscuits I get at the pet store. I also buy her flowers every week. A lot of my time is spent taking care of my giraffe. That's pretty much all I do.

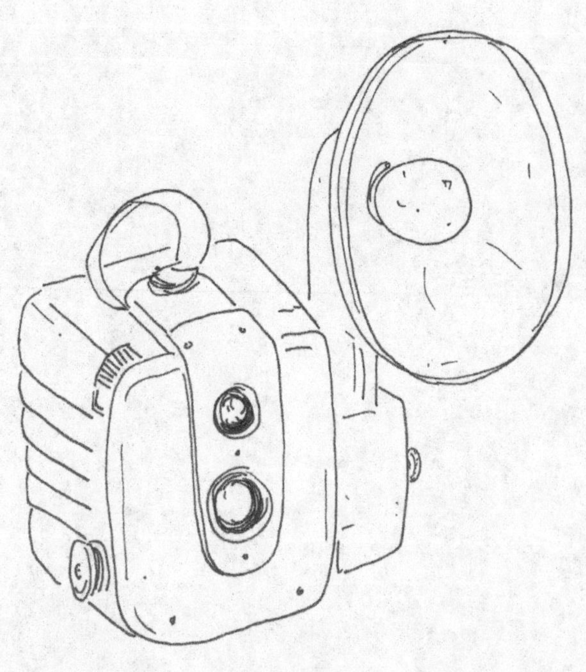

CHAPTER 2
BETTE DAVIS

Bette Davis once said, "I would not have married someone who could not support me." Not that I'm comparing Tulip to that Hollywood legend. They don't look that much alike. But I do think they share some of that same charismatic presence. Every time we step out, Tulip holds her head dignified, stopping occasionally to nuzzle the leaves. People still gather and take pictures. We don't mind their attention, she's a star after all.

That little altercation with the birthday party next door reminded me she needed to go for a walk. In the wild, I read she would walk eight or ten miles a day. That seems a bit extreme to me. We have some wooded paths we like to follow. They go along the creek, up around the high school, past the big spread of José's Garden where we often stop for a snack. Sometimes we cross Taylor Avenue, through campus to the top of the hill. We can see all of town from up there. Of course, Tulip can see most of town from anywhere she stands. Sometimes we take the Mill Avenue sidewalk, into town to the shore. There's a spot near the water where the blue herons nest in the trees. Tulip likes to visit them, peeking over the branches they've sewn together. They seem to share something in common. Like her, they move in the air silently, slow and elegant—neither animal seems entirely real.

A ladder leans against the house. She's used to me getting that clackety metal contraption. I set it beside her and climb. There was a time I had to chase her around the yard with it, now she knows it's just my way of becoming a giraffe, standing at the top of those rungs, petting her neck.

I offered her an apple and she let me put the leash on her. I don't take any chances being near the roads and I don't let her wander from me into anyone's summer flowers. I wait until we get to a field to release her. She needs that free time to remember what Africa was like.

I led Tulip out the backyard gate and she brushed her horns in the cottonwood leaves.

The girl from next door trotted into the alley to meet us. She left the party with a paper plate and held it up to Tulip. Half a piece of birthday cake.

"Oh, hello," I said. Tulip's long neck was coming down. "I don't think we better feed her that. But here…" I reached into my shoulder-bag and got a stalk of celery. "Would you like to give Tulip this?"

She did. She took the celery and Tulip swung in to eat it. The girl laughed. She wore a crown and a purple dress.

"Tulip says thank you," I said. "She loves celery and vegetables and fruit."

"And candy too," the girl told me.

"Yes," I laughed, "sorry about that. She probably thought your piñata was for her."

"I don't mind. It's my birthday and I like giraffes."

CHAPTER 3
WALKING with a GIRAFFE

Tulip clopped along the sidewalk. We did have to stop more and more often for her to sample the plums and apples growing along the way. Pears were ripe too. For her, food was everywhere. She must think the neighborhood is a kind of miracle to pick and choose. She gleaned along the top of the blackberry bushes where people couldn't reach. She sampled the maple leaves. I guess if you're tall as a giraffe, you need to eat all the time. That's just what they do.

As we went across the empty playing field of the elementary school, I could see the kids inside staring out the windows. I waved. The teacher glared. She was probably trying to teach them something important. I didn't want to interrupt them; this happens to be a shortcut we like to take. People in cars have their roads, while we can take any old way we want. Tulip was interested in the flag clanking on the pole as it flapped in the breeze. I wonder what she'd look like with flags running down her long neck. What if I tied a black pirate flag to her scruffy mane and put her on skates and dressed her in sails? Whoosh, she would fly away from me, I'd be running in her wake!

I told her we couldn't go far right now, I had work to do back at home. I suppose that's something kids get used to hearing too. I know she sees each visit outside as a chance to play, but I can't tarry about all day, I do have to make a living, that much is true. I told her at the end of the schoolgrounds that we would follow the path returning into trees. I'm sure she knows what I'm saying, though she doesn't like to hear it. We passed the swings, and the slide that looked like the skeleton of a giraffe bowing down. Dandelions dotted around us.

I never expected to be walking a giraffe on a leash. Now that I am, a couple of times every day, it's become my routine. When I make tea every morning, Tulip watches me through the screen window, waiting for us to go.

A squirrel chattered and ran from us down the branch of an oak. I would've thought all the animals of the forest knew us by now. They ought to. All we do is walk by. A blue jay made a yell. Tulip stopped at the crook where there used to be a honeybee hive. A memory like that doesn't easily melt away.

I heard a bicycle coming our way. I pulled the leash in.

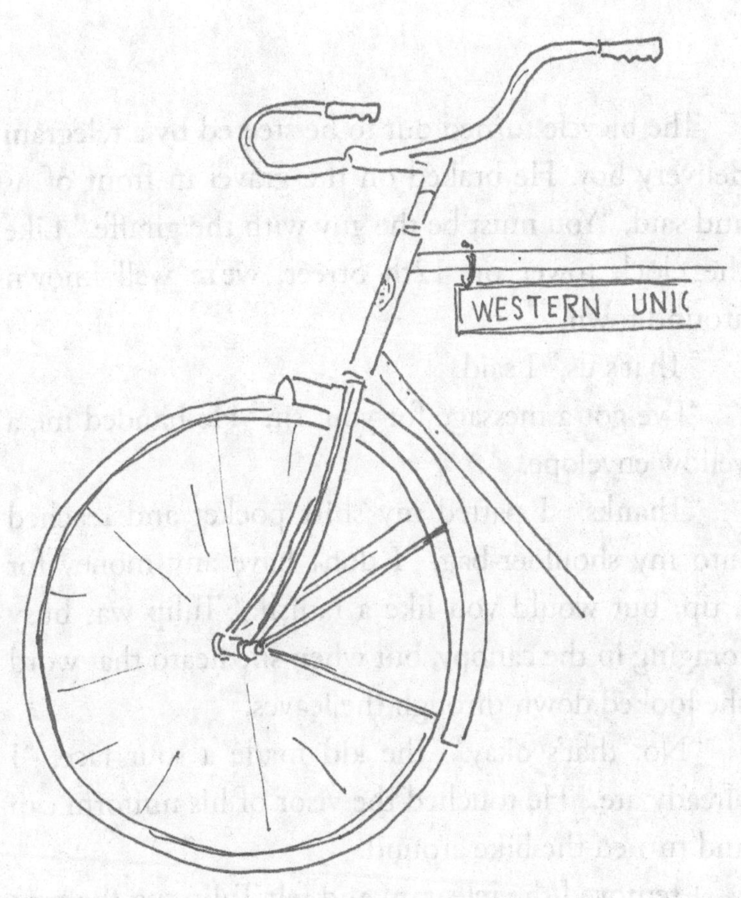

CHAPTER 4
WRAPPED in a CABBAGE LEAF

The bicycle turned out to be steered by a telegram delivery boy. He braked on the gravel in front of us and said, "You must be the guy with the giraffe." Like the clock tower on 12th Street, we're well known around town.

"That's us," I said.

"I've got a message for you, sir." He handed me a yellow envelope.

"Thanks." I patted my shirt pocket and reached into my shoulder-bag, "I don't have any money for a tip, but would you like a radish?" Tulip was busy foraging in the canopy, but when she heard that word she looked down through the leaves.

"No, that's okay." The kid made a sour face. "I already ate." He touched the visor of his uniform cap and turned the bike around.

I removed the telegram and felt Tulip tug the torn

yellow envelope from my other hand. She probably thought it was a cabbage leaf.

MR. VIRGIL CHEF

REQUEST YOUR PRESENCE AT OXFORD APARTMENTS WILL BE WAITING

TGC MARCONI

Interesting, I thought. I don't know anyone with that peculiar name. I do know The Oxford Apartments though. It isn't far from our house, it's on Harris Avenue. We could be there in ten minutes.

CHAPTER 5
A FORGOTTEN ISLAND

There are a few garbage dumpsters in the parking lot and the sort of cars you'd see at a used car lot for cheap. The Oxford Apartments is a two-story structure painted a peeling mossy green. An air conditioner propped in one of the first-floor windows wheezed. There weren't any kids playing jump rope on the sidewalk, no chalk drawings, no hopscotch, there wasn't anyone sitting in the sun on the stairway leading to the balcony. In fact, there were ominous signs on the stair railing:

> **WARNING**
> **Use Extreme Caution**
> **Watch Your Step**
> **During Construction**

It didn't seem like construction was happening

anytime soon. The Oxford Apartments looked like a forgotten island.

I looked around and decided to tie Tulip's leash to a pine tree beside the parking lot. Thankfully she's an easy-going animal. Her big brown eyes watched me as I walked around that rickety stairway and checked the tenant listing next to the mailboxes. Marconi's room was listed as 2D.

I stepped back and gave that stairway a quick inspection. From underneath, I could plainly see the missing steps and screws that were rusting through. Somehow, I'd have to climb that awful fabrication without falling to my doom. The thought did cross my mind of climbing on Tulip's back and having her deliver me to the balcony level. I don't know which choice would be more dangerous.

Nobody came running out to warn me not to do it, so I decided on the stairs. The railing wagged in my grip. I tested the first step, put some weight on it, heard it creak balefully as I left the cracked cement of the ground. There were some obvious places not to put your feet, jagged holes, and bent nails, but it seemed I was relying mostly on luck as I went up. Luck is something I seem to have on my side—how else could I have got a giraffe?

PRESSURE

CHAPTER 6
The NEXT GREAT HOUDINI

A robot answered the door, a metal man welded and bolted together with flashing lights for eyes. A dial spun on his chest, the arrow went round and round. "No solicitations at this time," it told me.

"No, I'm not selling anything," I promised. "I have a telegram that asked me to visit you. I'm Virgil Chef. Are you Marconi?"

The robot eased the door back open. "Hardly," it said. It made a scratchy sound that could have been laughter, or bad wiring. "My name is Cronco." It presented an iron claw and we shook hands carefully. "I believe your presence is expected. Follow me." Cronco shuffled and led the way. I don't know how it ever made it up the stairway. Maybe the Oxford has a freight elevator somewhere.

The apartment walls were covered with posters and framed photos. Apparently Cronco and Marconi were performers. A bright poster over the couch portrayed Cronco breathing fire while a magician held a levitating candelabra fixed in midair. I was still examining the walls when a gnomelike elderly man appeared from the kitchen. He wore an apron and was drying off a gravy bowl.

"Ahah!" he boomed, "You must be Virgil Chef."

I nodded.

He placed the towel over his shoulder and reached out a hand. "I'm pleased to meet you." His left hand held onto that gravy bowl like Aladdin's lamp. "As you have already noticed, my companion Cronco and I have a life upon the stage. And you can imagine, such a vocation places great demands upon us to constantly come up with acts of surprise and ingenuity. Regarding that, I understand you have a giraffe?"

"Yes," I said.

"How wonderful, how delightful. What an extraordinary fortuitous occurrence!"

I think I could tell what he was leading up to. He didn't come right out and say it yet, he was the type that had to paper something simple all over with words.

"Did you bring your giraffe with you?" Marconi asked.

"She goes everywhere with me. She's tied to a tree."

He hugged the gravy bowl and practically ran past me to the window. "She's marvelous!" he cried. I walked over and looked around the curtain too. The top of Tulip's head stared across the balcony. "I don't think you realize what you've got there. I don't think you've any idea at all!" He clutched my arm and announced, "This giraffe could be the next great Houdini!"

CHAPTER 7
CAULIFLOWER

I told him no. I see no reason for Tulip to be on stage. We don't go looking for anything more than what we already have, we're just fine with the world as it is, presented with a neighborhood of trees and paths we revisit every day. Marconi begged and promised a vision of spotlights in the sky, radio and television, and a mansion by the sea. I politely said no to each one of his dreams until finally he had to let me go. Cronco held the door for me. I was glad I didn't have to shake that claw again. I felt that I had upset them, but it was a basic misunderstanding. We have different views on what a giraffe is for.

The stairway gave me the same scare as before. Rocking and creaking. Each warning sign was one step closer to the earth. Seeing Tulip waiting for me, watching, gave me the courage I needed. With one last leap, I hurried to her, to the groundcover littered with pine needles and pinecones like fallen grenades. "Let's get out of here, Tulip," I whispered. As I untied the leash, she bent down and licked the back of my neck.

I didn't look back at The Oxford. I was pretty sure Marconi and Cronco were glaring from their window, I didn't want to see them again. It's a small town though. And my luck could only last so long.

As we walked, I dug into my shoulder-bag and got Tulip a cauliflower.

CHAPTER 8
WOODEN NICKELS

Tulip sleeps in our shady backyard. In case you're wondering, she can sleep standing up. She can also sleep lying down. I've never seen her try to sleep in the hammock though. After our walk, I expect her to nap at least half an hour. The little birds dart around her. Sometimes a wren will climb up those checkerboard markings on her skin. One time a sparrow tried to make a nest on her horns

This is a good time for me to get some work done. On the kitchen table is my assembly line. I've got a printmaking machine, and a big bag of blank wooden circles. I bet you've already guessed what I do with them. I make wooden nickels. I stamp them with whatever slogans or pictures my client wants. I customize them for drugstores, coffee shops, tourist traps and truck-stops. Today I'm making 100 coins for a joke shop in Des Moines, Iowa. I'm not the U.S.

Mint, but I do good business. I send them all over the country, all America needs a laugh.

My memory kept going back to that magician Marconi. I felt bad about letting him down. He really had his heart set on a giraffe. I wonder what he wanted Tulip to do. Maybe another animal will do the job. Maybe he'll find someone with a horse for rent. Some black and white paint would make it a zebra. If I happen to see him again, I'll suggest that. I could even paint if for him, I've had lots of experience counterfeiting.

CHAPTER 9
LUCKY (AGAIN)

A hundred wooden coins later, I taped them inside a cardboard box. Tulip was still asleep. Usually, we go the post office together. I didn't want to wake her though. She was all dappled in sunlight and shadows, calm as a postage stamp. So I left her there in the backyard. I shouldn't have. I didn't know it then. I wish I would've been more aware. How could I know what was going to happen? Do you?

That's just the way it goes, I guess.

Don't worry. I'll do my best. And as I already told you, luck is on my side.

Like I said, I left her there in the backyard. It wasn't that far to the post office. I rode my bike so I could be there and back before Tulip had any idea that I was gone.

Oh Tulip, I'm sorry! I didn't even say goodbye.

Mill Avenue turned into 13th Street, and I wheeled

onto the deer path that rattled downhill between the vacant lots. The sea shined blue ahead of me. The sun sparked white on it. The box in the basket jumped around. Only once did I have to keep it from flying out.

The post office is next to the laundromat which is next to a Mexican restaurant.

I was lucky (again) there was only one person ahead of me and it didn't take long for the package to begin its journey from here to Iowa.

"Where's your giraffe?" someone called to me outside.

I didn't recognize her, but when you walk around town with a giraffe people tend to identify you. "She's at home," I said.

"She likes flowers, doesn't she?"

"Yes," I said. And I was surprised as she reached back into her parked car and got a bouquet. People do things like this all the time, I shouldn't be surprised. A giraffe brings out the best in them.

"Do you think she'd like these?" she asked.

"I'm sure she would," I said. Tulip can't resist a bunch of daisies. "Thank you." I put them in the basket where the wooden nickels used to be.

CHAPTER 10
GIRAFFE on a RAFT

I never thought of life without Tulip. Why would I? Once we were together it felt like time stood still. We were in a photograph forever. I thought of getting home and her enjoying those daisies, eating them in a few bites. I would scratch her forehead and hug her and hear her three hearts beating. The dusk would be tuning down the day. I stopped by the library; it was just off Finnegan Way.

I left my bike in the brush, in the place I always do. Nobody but a deer looking for succulents would ever see it. And the shiny metal spokes would mean nothing to it. The daisies might, but I wouldn't be long. Anyway, I didn't see any deer around. I figured it was okay.

Any book about giraffes is a book for me.

After reading every one in the library, they've been helping me to reach out far and wide for more. I'm not picky—as long as there's a giraffe in it, I'm happy. This time it was a travel adventure loaned from the Euclid Public Library. Someone took a Mark Twain journey across Lake Erie and wrote *Giraffe on a Raft*. I flipped through it to the black and white photos in the middle. The author wearing a straw hat. The author chipping away at a log and another showing the raft in progress. A map of the lake with a dashed line indicating the intended route to Canada and back. A blurry scene that might have been the Loch Ness monster. I didn't want to spoil the adventure that lay ahead so I shut the book and tucked it under my arm. I could read it soon enough I thought, in the hammock with Tulip holding a lantern next to me.

CHAPTER 11
EMPTY

When I got back home, I pushed the bike over the bumpy, weedy driveway. A shadow of us blued along the side of the house. Usually, if she's not with me, Tulip listens for me and she'll be there at the gate. The gate was open though. That was the first clue that something might be wrong.

As you can imagine, I'm always careful to lock the gate. There's no way that latch could snap by itself. "Tulip!" I called. I was trying not to conjure a nightmare. I wanted to see her awakening, blinking beside the tree.

"Tulip!" The backyard was empty. I dropped my bicycle and the book spilled out of the basket. I didn't see any sign of her.

A whirlpool swirled in the air and took my world away. I was steering with all my might not to drop into it.

I ran past my bike, out the gate again and the driveway, past my parked pickup truck. I couldn't think of driving it without her.

I wanted to see Tulip across the street, browsing the neighbor's hawthorn tree, or see her loping along up Mill. But you've never seen such an empty landscape. I could've been on Mars. I didn't know what else to do. She had been erased from my universe.

Would it make sense to call the police? It was hard to believe they would take me seriously, that they would send out a fleet of squad cars in search of a giraffe.

Then I remembered Tony Epsilon.

CHAPTER 12
TONY EPSILON

"Tony Epsilon, private eye," said the voice in my ear.

"Hello, Tony. This is Virgil Chef." There was a pause until I clarified, "We met at the vet's office. Your parrot had laryngitis. You gave me your card and said to call if I ever needed a detective."

"Virgil Chef!" he cried. "Of course! You have a giraffe."

"*Had* a giraffe. I don't know what happened to her, she's gone." I took a breath and told him the story.

"Can you think of anyone who would want to take your giraffe?" he asked me when I finished.

First, I thought of my next-door neighbor. Rocko called Tulip a menace today. He was angry but he's not the sort to do her harm. He's adapted to life with a giraffe on the other side of his fence. I wondered if there was someone along our daily travels who's been plotting revenge. Maybe a gardener who lost too many zinnias to her passing through. I try to keep watch, but she does love flowers. It was hard to envision anyone ruthless enough to take her away. I mean, I know things like this happen, I know it can be a cruel world. That's when I recalled The Oxford Apartments and the man who lived there. "Oh no…" I said, "I just thought of someone."

CHAPTER 13
MARGIE

Tony insisted on going there. He arrived at my house in fifteen minutes. It was already night. His car rumbled at the curb and I got in. While he drove, I looked out the window. Every tall tree silhouette resembled a giraffe. If only one of them was Tulip.

"Don't worry," Tony said. "We'll find her."

"We'll find her," repeated the parrot riding on his shoulder.

Tony nodded, "That's right, Margie."

Like I said, I've met Margie before. I wasn't surprised to see her accompanying him, even if we were going into what might be a dangerous situation with a robot and a maniac magician. We are known for the animals we have with us. When people see me, they look for my giraffe. I only hope we can get her back.

On Harris Avenue I told Tony the apartments were

coming up.

"We'll find her," Margie echoed.

"Thanks, Margie," I said.

Tony read the wooden sign stuck by the road, "The Oxford Apartments…" and turned the steering wheel. The headlights shined briefly on the building as he parked. That was long enough for me to see the drastic change that occurred. The stairway had collapsed. It was crumpled in a pile of tangled wood and metal. The parking lot lamppost cast a ghoulish green light on the scene.

Tony said, "What do you suppose happened here?"

"I could hazard a guess," I said. It seemed pretty obvious. "The robot must have tried walking down."

"Which room is theirs?"

I pointed at 2D. It was the only set of windows with no lights on.

Tony shook his head. "Sure looks like they split." Then he held his hand like an elevator next to his shoulder. "Margie, why don't you go take a look." As she crawled onto his opened palm, with his left hand he unrolled the window and he let her out.

We watched her flutter and climb in the air to the second floor. In the dark by the window, she landed on the sill. She bobbed along it to an opening in the curtain. That was where we looked out before, Marconi and me. God, I never should have gone up there.

Tony said, "Here she comes…" and pushed his arm out the window. He made it look effortless, catching her like Joe DiMaggio. He brought her inside and set her on his knee. We were lucky she didn't have laryngitis anymore. We needed to hear what she saw.

She ruffled her wings and told us in two words, "Nobody's home!"

CHAPTER 14
ON SUCH a NIGHT

"I don't suppose you accept wooden nickels as pay?" I said. I wasn't trying to be rude, I just don't have much cash on hand.

Fortunately for me, Tony Epsilon is one of those Philip Marlowe kinds of detectives who live by an unspoken rule of chivalry. He shook his head and said, "Until I find your giraffe, I haven't done my job."

I didn't know what else to say. It had been a long day. I opened the car door and as I got out, I heard the parrot promise me, "We'll find her." I felt better about tomorrow. I stood beside the curb and watched their car grumble up Mill Avenue until the red taillights took it away.

I was anchored on the sidewalk thinking about Tulip until I decided to go check the backyard. What if someone brought her back? Or what if she just ambled out on her own and then sauntered in the gate? Wouldn't that be a lark?

The driveway was dark except for the part where the kitchen window light glowed down. It made the weeds and crumpled grass look like skeletons of what they were. The pickup carried a polished glint of electricity. It was a warm summer night. A giraffe would be pleased sleeping in a backyard on such a night.

CHAPTER 15
MERMAID POSTCARDS

The morning sky was cloudy and white. I could feel the cool air coming in the open window and it brought the smell of the ocean, carried like suitcases full of seaweed. Welcome to my little hotel, half a mile from the shore. Mermaids can explore the land like Hans Christian Andersen writing postcards at my kitchen table.

I didn't sleep very well. How could I? Still, after all the nightmares, I felt sure I would find Tulip today. You can't just whisk a giraffe away. Someone must have seen something. There was a lot to do. I got out of bed, got dressed, and made a bowl of oatmeal.

In one of my dreams, Tulip wasn't gone. I found her in the backyard by accident, good as ever, only she was the size of a caterpillar. I cupped her out of the grass in my hands. I know it sounds improbable, but in dreams anything can happen, and sometimes I've seen them work out to be true. So as the coffee was brewing, I went outside and searched the backyard.

What kind of fairytale was I falling into? After a few minutes getting dew on my feet, I returned to my breakfast. I sat with my money factory and a coffee cup in my hand. I looked at the words I wrote on a piece of paper. It also had a photograph of my giraffe taped on. I'm sure you've seen flyers like this stapled to telephone poles, only this wasn't for a Lost Cat or Lost Dog. At the bottom of the page, I wrote in black pen: CALL FOR REWARD. I was prepared to give every wooden nickel I owned.

CHAPTER 16
In the RUBBLE

After a quick stop at the Quick Stop photocopy shop, I had fifty copies of my LOST GIRAFFE poster. While I pedaled to Harris Avenue, I stopped people on the street and told them about Tulip. I stopped at cafés and stores, and I tacked them up wherever I could. It was difficult to believe that nobody had seen a fifteen-foot creature in their midst. From their expressions you'd think I was talking about a unicorn. On the corner of 21st I left a flyer with the cashier at the market. The Oxford Apartments were in sight, they were slumped across the street.

The building didn't look any better during the day. There was still a pile of broken staircase bones. I don't know how people were getting to and from the second floor. A vine like Tarzan's perhaps.

I walked carefully around the splinters, on my way to the mailboxes, and noticed something in the rubble that didn't belong to mere shoddy construction. I had seen it before…upstairs…in 2D…It was the lower half of a robot's leg, broken free from the knee down. It was pinned in with the twisted carnage, not that I was about to clamber on the pile and try and retrieve it; my giraffe story was already met with disbelief, why add to the aversion by carrying a robot's leg too?

At any rate, the sight of it was enough to confirm my suspicions. Here's what I think happened: Marconi waited until we were out of sight. Then he decided to follow us, to see where we lived. He made it down the stairs, just as I had, only he was a magician, he could have used the Indian Rope Trick to descend. But urging his weighty robot companion to follow was a different matter. One step onto the stairs and Cronco was crashing to the ground. Marconi would have helped his disabled friend, but he would have been anxious to hurry, as we were probably nearing 22nd Street by then. So, they left the rest of its leg buried and got in one of those unfortunate vehicles that leaned about the lot. I didn't notice anyone following us, but that must be what happened. They watched me put Tulip in the backyard and they waited for the right time and when I left the house on my bicycle, they had their chance.

"Hey!" a woman called from the balcony above me.

I turned and looked at her. She held on in the air like Juliet with a cigarette. I asked, "Me?"

"Yeah. Are you here to fix the stairs?"

"No. I'm—"

"You got a sandwich or something to eat? I'm starving."

"No, I'm sorry, I—"

"Can yet get help? There's no way down from here."

"Okay," I promised. "I'll do what I can." There's always someone else with problems too.

CHAPTER 17
BETTER DAYS

How do you get through times like this? I remembered better days. I remembered driving Tulip to the park. She had a seatbelt to wear in the back of the truck. As I drove, she would lean her head forward, over the cab, and I could see her long neck as she ruffled in the wind. That was good practice, as we slowed, approached the aqueduct underpass, she stayed low through the arch made of stones. Then her head would pop back up like a periscope. She was interested in the people playing ball, the dogs running after frisbees, the kids flying kites. One time she stretched across to the sidewalk and took an ice-cream cone from a vendor's cart. She could have been the star of a cartoon. I have enough stories to fill a book.

A couple weeks ago, I took her to the Moonlite Drive-In theater. The cars were parked in rows. A deep night sky overhead. The big movie screen at the front of the field was filled with Technicolor. And there in the middle of the movie was a giraffe silhouette.

Getting Tulip past the flower shop was comical. She would plant her legs like stilts, and it was impossible to pull her. W.C. Fields had better luck with an ostrich. Fortunately, the owner kept anything that had wilted or lost its bloom in a box labeled *Giraffe*. Tulip would gladly follow that to the end of the block. And you'd be surprised at the meals she would get: lilacs, roses, lavender, hibiscus, daisies, and marigolds. An orchid for dessert.

And I liked those lazy afternoons when we'd get home from our walk, when she would rest her chin on the walnut tree while I read a book in the hammock below. It wouldn't take very long…yawning, reading the same sentence over again, hearing the birds and the girl next door practicing piano…before the old sandman would putter along, across the grass with a handful of magic sleeping dust.

CHAPTER 18
NOTES in a SONG

Part of the problem was knowing where to find a vintage magician and his robot. How far can they go? How far can a one-legged robot get? I can't believe I'm even contemplating that.

But that's the reason I was pedaling town with a handful of flyers in my bicycle basket. They were nearly gone, but I wanted to save a few for Mill Avenue around my block.

The Black Spot coffee shop took one and then as I was crossing the street pushing my bike, I had a lucky break.

When you've got an eye for posters you become attuned. They get placed like notes in a song. This one was a high C, ringing like a chime at the top of a bus stop sign.

TONIGHT ONLY!
SEE
The Great Colonel Marconi MAGIC Act
At the Avalon Vaudeville Theatre
WHAT will he saw in half??

"Oh no!" I groaned. Poor Tulip! I turned onto Champion Street and rode like the wind.

T MISFIT SHOW
74181

CHAPTER 19
The GIRAFFE COMEDIAN

There's an alley that runs behind the Avalon. I had to squeeze past a bus for The Traveling Misfit Puppet Show. I figured they were also on the bill tonight. I didn't want to disturb them. I was looking for a stage door. I just wanted to sneak in for a minute and see if Marconi was in.

I leaned my bicycle against the brick wall beside a garbage can. It seemed a safe place, puppets can't ride a bicycle, can they? Their strings would tangle in the spokes and chain. An orange book left on the lid of the bin caught my attention. Stamped in blue letters on the cover was the title: *The Humor Thesaurus*. I picked it up and thumbed some pages. It was thick, a bit waterlogged, and even at an arm's length I could smell the musty clamor of the yellow newsprint pulp. Jokes compiled by subject matter filled 600 pages. Furniture, Trains, Sleep…I flipped to the front and saw there was a section for Animals. I didn't have time to look for my favorite topic, so I tossed the book into my bike basket for later.

Painted across the stage door was a warning: FOR ACTORS AND EMPLOYEES ONLY. It was okay, I was here to save my giraffe.

I pulled on the handle and saw a wooden hallway with set pieces and stage-drops lining the walls between doors. I walked in past a landscape full of trees and a castle on a hill. On the other side of me was a painting of the seashore. Either way I turned I'd be in a different world. I passed the lighthouse when someone came out of a door on my left. The room smelled like the air inside of a bicycle tire.

He wore blue overalls and carried a pail. A cigar was screwed in his face. "What you doing here?" he asked. He looked a little like Adolphe Menjou. If Adolphe Menjou gave up the life of an aristocrat to become a janitor. "Turn around. This here's just for the talent."

"I know," I said, and I don't know how it came to me so suddenly as I added, "I do jokes." I said, "I'm in the show tonight."

"Is that so?"

I nodded. "I'm…The Giraffe Comedian."

He blinked and bore down on the cigar. "I don't recollect that," he puffed. "You on the roster?"

"I should be."

He got a scrap of paper from his pocket and examined it. Then he wrote my name down and told me to come back tonight.

And just like that, I became part of showbiz history.

CHAPTER 20
SPOKANE

What luck it was finding that book! If Tulip could hold on a little longer, I would be rescuing her tonight. I was third on the billing, not bad right? I was on after a father-daughter clog-dancing routine. Now, all I needed to do was come up with my act. I am terrible at telling jokes. I'm well aware it's something best left to the professionals, but I had an ace up my sleeve. The book rattled in my basket with every weal on the tar. I glided on Mill until my house reappeared. Bumped up the driveway, I parked and took my joke book and flyers to the front door.

A folded note had been stuffed in the jamb.

A flurry of new worries ran about in my mind, but it might also be good news I told myself.

I removed it and unfolded it and turned it around and read it.

Virgil
We stopped by. No sign of you.
We got a tip about your better half. We're going to
Spokane to check it out.
Will let you know.
Margie says not to worry, we'll find her.
Tony E.

Spokane?

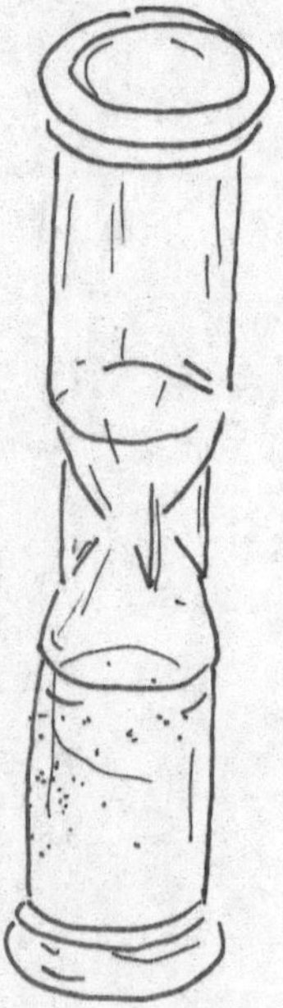

CHAPTER 21
SAND

I needed to fill five minutes. That doesn't sound like a lot. But I felt like I was in high school again, trying to do a report. It didn't take me long to realize the thesaurus belonged to that garbage can. The so-called jokes were dry as papyrus. I spent an hour at the kitchen table, trying desperately to make something out of sand. With any luck I would get booed off the stage. Actually, that wasn't a bad proposition. That would allow me to find Tulip all the sooner…As long as they didn't toss me out into the alley.

I drummed my fingers on the cover and opened it again. The book was from 1940, the Golden Age of Comedy. I know they had some great entertainment then—Jack Benny, Phil Harris, Fred Allen, Our Miss Brooks, The Bob Hope Show—they were all on the radio. So why weren't they reaching out across time to lend me a hand? Five minutes never seemed like such a desert. I was looking for an oasis, but I'd settle for a mirage.

CHAPTER 22
ANOTHER JOKE

Jokes weren't the only thing I needed to prepare. I took a break from the tabletop Sahara and went to my room. I only have one suit. I don't often wear it. I can't remember the last time I needed to. I carried it to the backyard and hung it on the wash line. It was dark blue, but it wouldn't be for long. I returned to the house and looked for paint.

I'm sure everyone ends up with a stack of cans from leftover projects and you don't ever seem to be able to use it all and then it dries. The life of a lowly paint can. But I do need them on hand. I never know when I might need another color for my wooden coins. If Saint Patrick's Day is near and I don't have any green, I'm in trouble. A blue shamrock won't do.

I got a can of yellow paint and a brush. I must have been inspired—on my way to the kitchen door, I stopped at the table and wrote another joke. One I thought up myself! It may not be published by Crown Printers Corporation in 1940, but I thought it was pretty good.

The backyard was lonesome to see, but tomorrow it wouldn't be.

I still had time, the sun was shining, I guess I had a solid five-minute set, and my suit was hanging like an empty canvas waiting for the paint.

CHAPTER 23
LUCILLE BALL

For all my painting prowess, did I consider how long a painted suit takes to dry? I regret to say, I did not. It wasn't a solid yellow—I kept the suit's original color for the patterned darker patches you see on a giraffe—still, there was enough wet paint on the coat and pants to worry me. The sun was getting lower, dipping into the trees. The Giraffe Comedian had found himself in a classic sitcom situation. I felt like Lucille Ball sneaking into the Tropicana Club.

Also, let's not forget, I had to memorize my material. I'm no actor. What was I supposed to do? I couldn't go out on the Avalon stage and read from a book. I needed an angle, something you'd see on *I Love Lucy.*

My jokes were written on cards. I considered stapling them to my sleeves, or I could write them on a long tie I could wheedle like Oliver Hardy. Then

I thought of a whole other scenario. One that didn't have to rely on a painted yellow suit. What if I played a grocer? What if I was The Supermarket Comedian? What if I had a table lined with groceries and what if I glued my jokes to the back of each box and jar and can?

Oh, I had to hand it to myself, it was ingenious! I had been blessed by a spark of comedy gold. Whatever angel or muse it was that spoke to the comedy greats had delivered a message channeled to me.

So I left my suit out in the yard where a giraffe belonged. If I needed a costume, it would be dry for Halloween.

CHAPTER 24
WENATCHEE

I gathered five minutes of groceries on my kitchen table. Each one had been ingeniously prepared, glued with a 1940s joke. I felt good about this now. I could get through this. I put everything in brown paper bags just like a real grocer would do. I got my white apron from the hook near the cupboards and put it on.

Then the telephone rang. It sits like a comfortable black cat on the ledge looking into the next room. I picked up the receiver and answered, "Hello?"

"Chef?"

"Yes."

"This is Tony Epsilon."

"Tony, where are you?"

"We're in Wenatchee."

"What about Spokane? What are you doing in Wenatchee?"

"It's a real nice town actually. It's on the way to

Spokane, but we might stay a while. We like it here."

"I thought you got a tip my giraffe is in Spokane?"

"Maybe…Maybe not…We're thinking not."

"Yeah, well I think I tracked her down. I think she's appearing tonight at the Avalon. In a magic act."

"That makes sense."

"I don't know what makes sense anymore. But I'll be there tonight, and I'll find out."

"Good," Tony said. "I hope this has a happy ending."

"Absolutely," I replied. "I'll sure be glad when it's over."

"You and me both," he said.

I told him, "Give my regards to Wenatchee."

"We already are."

He hung up and so did I.

CHAPTER 25
The SAME OLD LOVE SONG

Like I said, I felt good about my chances. I would perform—I didn't go through all this preparation for nothing—and who knows what might happen, why couldn't I dream of stardom? Then I would track down Tulip backstage and get her home safe and sound.

I brought the grocery bags to my truck and set them on the seat and floor. Do you think that author made it across Lake Erie on a raft with a giraffe without running into obstacles? We're a tough breed, we'll get by. You better believe it.

It was time to go.

Long shadows spread across purple Mill Avenue. The sun was nearly gone. I like this time of night. I like it even more knowing I'm on my way to rescue Tulip. When this old truck returns, she'll be riding with me, bowing under the maple trees and wires.

I turned on the dashboard radio and it was the same old love song a hundred million people played before.

CHAPTER 26
The SUPERMARKET COMEDIAN

One thing I didn't expect was how nervous I would be. The closer I got to the Avalon, I felt like a bee returning to the hive, bumbling and trembling at the door. I held my paper bags like pollen weighing me down.

Adolphe Menjou was there to meet me. He remembered me too. I could've used a memory like that for my act. "Hey Giraffe!" he barked at me. "You're cutting it close. You're on in five."

I set a bag down to wipe my brow. "Um…I'm not The Giraffe Comedian anymore."

"What? What did you say?"

"The Supermarket Comedian. That's my new name."

"Fine," he said. "I'll alert the *Herald*. Now get ready to go! Stage is that way."

I hurried along the hall, past the dressing rooms and

in the open doors I saw dancing girls, a ventriloquist argument, a juggler, and someone talking to a plant, but no sign of Marconi and his robot. I didn't see how they could get a giraffe into this place to begin with.

A hooflike racket beckoned me to the curtains offstage. If you've never heard two people dancing in clogs, the sound doesn't exactly help calm the nerves.

A man in a blue tuxedo stepped back from the curtain folds and approached me. He sneered at my appearance. "You the giraffe act?" he hissed.

"No, not anymore. I'm The Supermarket Comedian."

"The Supermarket Comedian," he repeated as if reading the toe-tag on a corpse. "Wait here for my introduction, then go to the spotlight."

"Oh, can I get a table? I need it for my props." I shook the grocery bags.

"I'll see if we can find you one."

So I stood there in the shadows and waited. I didn't feel so bad. I already survived my worst audience.

CHAPTER 27
The ACT

"And now, for his first appearance at the Avalon, please welcome a fresh new talent, The Supermarket Comedian!"

It happened too fast to worry anymore. I walked from the shadows, heard a scattered applause greeting me, not quite as loud as the squeaking old boards of the stage and I swung the paper bags jauntily. There was a lot of darkness around me, but I went right to the light and stopped in its glow beside the table, ready for me.

The introduction to *The Humor Thesaurus* serves as a guide for those who want to perform. It explains that the most difficult thing for a new comedian is simply getting on the stage for the first time. Once there, you want to immediately make that stage your own.

I said, "Hello everyone…" and I placed my grocery

bags on the table. "You may have seen me before at my day job." I reached into the first bag and took out a box of cereal. The thesaurus urges the comedy recruit to quickly get to the first joke. My first joke was supposed to be on the back of a box of bran flakes.

It wasn't.

I placed the box on the table and reached for another joke.

"Aha!" I said, "A can of pears!" but as I spun it, there was nothing funny attached to the wrapper.

The Humor Thesaurus is insistent, "The audience has to connect with you in the first minute. If they're not on your side, you will be facing an uphill battle."

I plunged my hand into another bag and it was the same problem. Just a box of detergent. Then another jar, of unfunny spaghetti. Where were my jokes?

I had nothing!

CHAPTER 28
WHAT HAPPENED

Here's what happened. I suppose in hindsight, it's laughable. It also turned out to be one of the oldest jokes, worthy of The Red Skelton Show or Harold Lloyd. A few months ago, I was at The Dollar Store where I traded a bag of wooden coins for some glue. They say you get what you pay for, and it's probably true.

You don't need me to tell you what happened, but in case you're unfamiliar with the comedy of the last 100 years, that bargain bin glue I used unpeeled. I wasn't aware there was a scrapheap of jokes lining each paper bag. So, I had to improvise. I ended my act reading the ingredients for a can of soup. Surprisingly that took three minutes. And it didn't get a single laugh.

I bombed. Humor is magic you can't learn from a book. When the curtains were finally drawn, I followed my table offstage, wishing it was a magic carpet instead. I could say, "Take me to Tahiti, or anywhere far away." But I still had something to do. I wasn't going to leave without Tulip.

CHAPTER 29
BUCK ROGERS

Cronco the robot stood in the hallway like an old icebox someone was getting rid of. Right away I noticed it was standing on a wooden leg, part of a solid antique oak desk, I would guess. I carried my shopping bags to where it guarded the door. "Hello, Cronco," I said.

Its eyes flickered.

"I need my giraffe."

Its clawed hands were folded across its chest but now they moved. I was prepared for the worst.

I continued, "Is this room where you're hiding her?"

"There is no giraffe in the vicinity," Cronco monotoned.

"Maybe not in this hallway, but I think you've got Tulip in there," I said and then like Buck Rogers I lunged around that massive robot and reached for the door handle.

It wasn't difficult for Cronco to lean into my way. My hands were tangled full of shopping bags.

Cronco warned me, "Mr. Marconi does not wish to be disturbed. He is running through his act."

"Running through his act with a *saw*, right?"

Cronco paused. "That is correct. However, the nature of the act must remain a secret until it is performed. My orders are that nobody is allowed in."

"Listen, Cronco," I pleaded, "That giraffe means the world to me. I would do anything for her."

"Apparently you would…" Cronco said. "I saw your act." And with that, a claw opened the door for me.

CHAPTER 30
A MIXED-UP WORLD

The Great Colonel Marconi tottered on one leg. His right leg was up on a table, encased in a wooden box like a sarcophagus painted with Egyptian and magical symbols. His foot poked out the far end of it. His toes wriggled. He had an evil-looking saw in his hand.

No sign of Tulip. The small room was cluttered with odd magic act implements and let's face it, you couldn't get a giraffe in here anyway. Even if you managed to squeeze her through the door, she would be stooped and bowed, contorted as a girl in a magician's trunk.

"Salutations, Mr. Chef," Marconi said. "To what calamitous occasion do we owe your interruption?"

"I'm looking for my giraffe." I didn't sound quite so heroic. "Someone took her."

Marconi seemed genuinely startled. "That's terrible

news indeed!"

My eyes roamed the room. I still couldn't believe she wasn't behind a coatrack or something. Maybe there was a trapdoor.

"I assure you there's no giraffe in here," Marconi told me. "Isn't that right, Cronco?"

"Affirmative," Cronco said.

The old magician crooked an eyebrow at me, "And Cronco cannot tell a lie."

I sighed. Suddenly the shopping bags were dragging me to the bottom of the sea. "I thought you took her," I admitted.

"You cut me to the quick!" he scolded me. "We are not common thieves!"

"I'm sorry, I can be so naive. I think this world is a beautiful dream and then something bad happens and I feel like a flower run over by a stampede."

"Flapdoodle!" Marconi exclaimed. "You can do bad too—you barged in here and blamed me for the loss of your giraffe! A scurrilous statement—and talk about bad, that act of yours out there!" he pointed towards the stage and held his nose. "No, it's a mixed-up world we're part of. But there are rules. Not everyone abides, but I think in here…" he tapped his heart, "We all know what they are."

"I hope so."

Marconi set his saw on top of his encased leg. "The loss of that magnificent animal is a catastrophe, but I believe providence has guided you here for an answer. I suggest you try the fortune-teller, Countess Netinkama. She's down two doors to the right."

I said, "Thank you, Mr. Marconi."

"The Great Colonel Marconi," Cronco piped up.

"It has been my pleasure," Marconi replied and bowed best he could.

"And good luck tonight sawing your leg in half," I said.

Before I left the room, Marconi offered me one last bit of advice. "Don't quit your day job."

CHAPTER 31
A DREAM WORD

I didn't get far into the hallway, I was shutting the door, avoiding a costumed cow, when I heard my name.

"Virgil Chef? Excuse me."

She didn't look like one of the Avalon regulars. She wore a gray business suit and she smiled. "I saw your act," she began.

"Oh no…"

"I was impressed. I think you have real talent."

"What?"

"I really do," she persisted. "I'd like to give you my card."

She handed it to me and I held it.

"I'd like to represent you," she said. "I don't know if you already have an agent?"

I read the swimming little words on the card. I didn't have my glasses, but it looked like:

DELLADELASCHENECTADYDIDIAS.

A dream word if ever I saw one. "I'm not sure what to say..."

She touched my arm, "Don't worry, you take your time." I wasn't aware if she said anything more, I had my head in the clouds just thinking about it.

CHAPTER 32
The SIGN of the ORACLE

I knocked on the door with the paper moon. Countess Netinkama answered right away, as if she had been waiting for me to get there and maybe she had. I don't know how much fortune-tellers can predict, or how their thoughts work. Their minds must be a loom with the past, present and future weaving all about.

She invited me to her table and I sat across from her. The dress she wore was like a cocoon on the chair, covered in a gauze of stars.

"You're looking for something or someone dear to you," she guessed.

"Yes."

She put one hand on the crystal ball and the other to her forehead and shut her eyes.

"I lost my giraffe," I whispered.

She nodded. She was in a place where she already knew that. She was a bird overhead, roving the dark city, searching every wooded copse and backyard. Parking lots, roundabouts. She could call out on imperceptible telegraph wires. She could read the tracks left on the moonlit ground. She laughed.

I hoped that was a good sign.

I almost asked her aloud, but I didn't want to break that trance she was in. Countess Netinkama might be holding on tightly to that crystal ball like a balloon floating her in the clouds. Her spirit needed time to near Champion Street again and reenter the little dressing room we sat in. She came back of her own accord.

When she opened her eyes, she told me, "You can go home now."

CHAPTER 33
SOME OTHER SYMPHONY

I can go home now. Thanks. I will. I returned to my truck and tossed the groceries inside the cab. They weren't just props—they were everything I had. My cupboards were bare without them. Me and Old Mother Hubbard had that in common. That and living in a fractured fairytale world.

Driving the dark road in and out of the streetlight glows, I listened to the radio.

The airwaves are full all the time with static, or mariachi, or some other symphony.

I wondered about the antennas stuck on roofs, and if those tip-top thoughts of Tulip might have been read by the fortune-teller. "You can go home now." I hope she told Tulip the same thing.

CHAPTER 34
HOME

No giraffe met me in the driveway. No eyes glowing in the headlights, staring over the gate. I collected my groceries and went in my house. No note on the door this time either. I left all those bags on the kitchen table and opened the door to the backyard. The light from the kitchen window made a yellow square in the black. I walked around in the grass, enough to know Tulip wasn't hiding.

The tinny sound of a toy piano played next door.

An airplane crossed the night sky. All I could see were stars and the shadow of the tree.

"Go home," the fortune-teller told me. What was going to happen? Was Tulip going to parachute from that plane?

I untied the strings of my apron and pulled it off and crumpled it. The Supermarket Comedian was home and didn't know what to do.

Was I supposed to call the name on that business card? I don't know if I could be funny again. How do they do it—those comedians we watch on TV— when some tragedy happens in their lives, how do they go on? Honestly, I don't know how funny I was to begin with, I don't know what she saw in me. The Supermarket Comedian was only here to get me through a day.

Maybe I would call her anyway.

I liked her smile.

CHAPTER 35
The SLEEPOVER

I was putting my groceries away in the cupboards when I heard the doorbell.

I didn't know what was going to happen next, this adventure had opened me up to all sorts of unforeseen events. The porchlight was on. I could see my neighbor Rocko. At least he didn't look upset this time.

"Evening Virgil," he said when I opened the door. He held his baseball cap in his hands. "I saw the sign you made for your giraffe. I think you better follow me."

He backed down the steps and I walked with him around the rhododendron onto his gravel driveway. "What is it?" I asked.

"You'll see," he said. "My daughter has something to tell you."

Now I was worried. Who wouldn't be?

He paused at the latch to his backyard and said,

"I was so glad she was finally eating all her vegetables. I had to go to the supermarket and get more. Cabbages, carrots, cantaloupes, I don't know what else. I couldn't believe that kid's appetite!"

With a click, he opened the gate. The birthday party kids were gone, but the big tent was still up and a lantern in it shimmered, along with the toy piano song and the shadow of a giraffe.

"It's crazy!" Rocko said, "I didn't know she was feeding your giraffe!"

I wanted to run around him.

Rocko shoed a beachball out of the way. "I swear I didn't know anything about it. My daughter's been hiding it in there for a couple days." He turned to me in the dim light and said, "I'm sorry for all the trouble," then he moved the flap aside and there they were.

Together, the girl next door and Tulip kneeled on blankets and pillows, next to the piano. Tulip knew it was me, but she was playing it cool.

Finished August 19, 2021
7:22 PM

Cover of *Pie in the Sky #72*, 1993

AFTERWORD

There's something about giraffes that has attracted me all my life. I suppose if I get reincarnated as one, I won't be surprised. Or maybe I already made it through that rite of passage. If being human is the top of the chain. Sometimes I wonder.

I was walking South Hill with Aaron in early August, and we like to stop at the free book kiosks. There are quite a few of them scattered around town. I don't have much luck catching good books this way, but that random thrill is part of what makes us stop. One time I found *Zen Mind, Beginner's Mind* by Suzuki. This day, I found a *Thesaurus of Humor*. I knew it would work its way into the new giraffe book I was contemplating.

This little book only took a few weeks to write. It was too hot to go outside, and the forests were burning, smoking up the sky. A red sun in the day, at night a red moon. A giraffe got me through.

HALF A GIRAFFE

written during August 2021

Books by Good Deed Rain

Saint Lemonade, Allen Frost, 2014. Two novels illustrated by the author in the manner of the old Big Little Books.

Playground, Allen Frost, 2014. Poems collected from seven years of chapbooks.

Roosevelt, Allen Frost, 2015. A Pacific Northwest novel set in July, 1942, when a boy and a girl search for a missing elephant. Illustrated throughout by Fred Sodt.

5 Novels, Allen Frost, 2015. Novels written over five years, featuring circus giants, clockwork animals, detectives and time travelers.

The Sylvan Moore Show, Allen Frost, 2015. A short story omnibus of 193 stories written over 30 years.

Town in a Cloud, Allen Frost, 2015. A three part book of poetry, written during the Bellingham rainy seasons of fall, winter, and spring.

A Flutter of Birds Passing Through Heaven: A Tribute to Robert Sund, 2016. Edited by Allen Frost and Paul Piper. The story of a legendary Ish River poet & artist.

At the Edge of America, Allen Frost, 2016. Two novels in one book blend time travel in a mythical poetic America.

Lake Erie Submarine, Allen Frost, 2016. A two week vacation in Ohio inspired these poems, illustrated by the author.

and Light, Paul Piper, 2016. Poetry written over three years. Illustrated with watercolors by Penny Piper.

The Book of Ticks, Allen Frost, 2017. A giant collection of 8 mysterious adventures featuring Phil Ticks. Illustrated throughout by Aaron Gunderson.

I Can Only Imagine, Allen Frost, 2017. Five adventures of love and heartbreak dreamed in an imaginary world. Cover & color illustrations by Annabelle Barrett.

The Orphanage of Abandoned Teenagers, Allen Frost, 2017. A fictional guide for teens and their parents. Illustrated by the author.

In the Valley of Mystic Light: An Oral History of the Skagit Valley Arts Scene, 2017. A comprehensive illustrated tribute. Edited by Claire Swedberg & Rita Hupy.

Different Planet, Allen Frost, 2017. Four science fiction adventures: reincarnation, robots, talking animals, outer space and clones. Cover & illustrations by Laura Vasyutynska.

Go with the Flow: A Tribute to Clyde Sanborn, 2018. Edited by Allen Frost. The life and art of a timeless river poet. In beautiful living color!

Homeless Sutra, Allen Frost, 2018. Four stories: Sylvan Moore, a flying monk, a water salesman, and a guardian rabbit.

The Lake Walker, Allen Frost 2018. A little novel set in black and white like one of those old European movies about death and life.

A Hundred Dreams Ago, Allen Frost, 2018. A winter book of poetry and prose. Illustrated by Aaron Gunderson.

Almost Animals, Allen Frost, 2018. A collection of linked stories, thinking about what makes us animals.

The Robotic Age, Allen Frost, 2018. A vaudeville magician and his faithful robot track down ghosts. Illustrated throughout by Aaron Gunderson.

Kennedy, Allen Frost, 2018. This sequel to *Roosevelt* is a coming-of-age fable set during two weeks in 1962 in a mythical Kennedyland. Illustrated throughout by Fred Sodt.

Fable, Allen Frost, 2018. There's something going on in this country and I can best relate it in fable: the parable of the rabbits, a bedtime story, and the diary of our trip to Ohio.

Elbows & Knees: Essays & Plays, Allen Frost, 2018. A thrilling collection of writing about some of my favorite subjects, from B-movies to Brautigan.

The Last Paper Stars, Allen Frost 2019. A trip back in time to the 20 year old mind of Frankenstein, and two other worlds of the future.

Walt Amherst is Awake, Allen Frost, 2019. The dreamlife of an office worker. Illustrated throughout by Aaron Gunderson.

When You Smile You Let in Light, Allen Frost, 2019. An atomic love story written by a 23 year old.

Pinocchio in America, Allen Frost, 2019. After 82 years buried underground, Pinocchio returns to life behind a car repair shop in America.

Taking Her Sides on Immortality, Robert Huff, 2019. The long awaited poetry collection from a local, nationally renowned master of words.

Florida, Allen Frost, 2019. Three days in Florida turned into a book of sunshine inspired stories.

Blue Anthem Wailing, Allen Frost, 2019. My first novel written in college is an apocalyptic, Old Testament race through American shadows while Amelia Earhart flies overhead.

The Welfare Office, Allen Frost, 2019. The animals go in and out of the office, leaving these stories as footprints.

Island Air, Allen Frost, 2019. A detective novel featuring haiku, a lost library book and streetsongs.

Imaginary Someone, Allen Frost, 2020. A fictional memoir featuring 45 years of inspirations and obstacles in the life of a writer.

Violet of the Silent Movies, Allen Frost, 2020. A collection of starry-eyed short story poems, illustrated by the author.

The Tin Can Telephone, Allen Frost, 2020. A childhood memory novel set in 1975 Seattle, illustrated by author like a coloring book.

Heaven Crayon, Allen Frost, 2020. How the author's first book Ohio Trio would look if printed as a Big Little Book. Illustrated by the author.

Old Salt, Allen Frost, 2020. Authors of a fake novel get chased by tigers. Illustrations by the author.

A Field of Cabbages, Allen Frost, 2020. The sequel to The Robotic Age finds our heroes in a race against time to save Sunny Jim's ghost. Illustrated by Aaron Gunderson.

River Road, Allen Frost, 2020. A paperboy delivers the news to a ghost town. Illustrated by the author.

The Puttering Marvel, Allen Frost, 2021. Eleven short stories with illustrations by the author.

Something Bright, Allen Frost, 2021. 106 short story poems walking with you from winter into spring. Illustrated by the author.

The Trillium Witch, Allen Frost, 2021. A detective novel about witches in the Pacific Northwest rain. Illustrated by the author.

Cosmonaut, Allen Frost, 2021. Yuri Gagarin stars in this novel that follows his rocket landing in an American town. Midnight jazz, folk music, mystery and sorcery. Illustrated by the author.

Thriftstore Madonna, Allen Frost, 2021. 124 summer story poems. Illustrated by the author.

Half a Giraffe, Allen Frost, 2021. A magical novel about a counterfeiter and his unusual, beloved pet. Illustrated by the author.

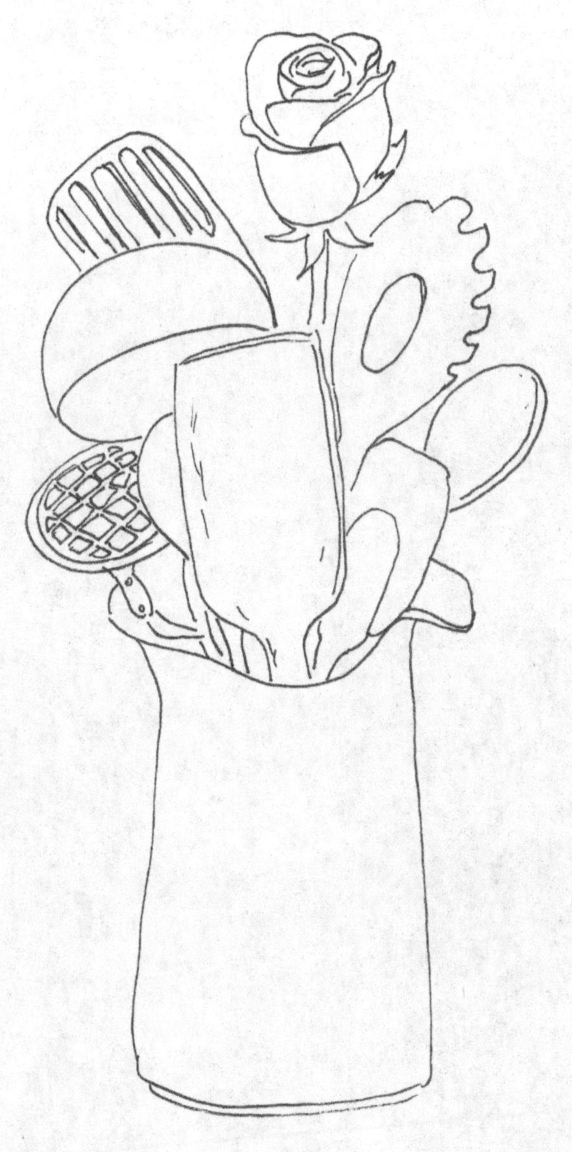

The author thanks giraffes everywhere

THESAURUS OF
HUMOR

www.ingramcontent.com/pod-product-compliance
Lightning Source LLC
Chambersburg PA
CBHW010511100726
47902CB00011B/2176